T0069777

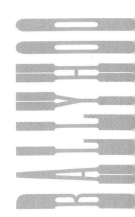

Johns Hopkins:
Poetry and Fiction

Wyatt Prunty,
General Editor

poems

by

hastings

hensel

Johns Hopkins
University Press
Baltimore

This book has been brought to publication with the generous assistance of the
John T. Irwin Poetry and Fiction Endowed Fund.

Printed in the United States of America on acid-free paper
9 8 7 6 5 4 3 2 1

Johns Hopkins University Press
2715 North Charles Street
Baltimore, Maryland 21218-4363
www.press.jhu.edu

Library of Congress Cataloging-in-Publication Data

Names: Hensel, Hastings, author.
Title: Ballyhoo / poems by Hastings Hensel.
Description: Baltimore : Johns Hopkins University Press, 2019. | Series: Johns
    Hopkins: poetry and fiction
Identifiers: LCCN 2018036807 | ISBN 9781421428758 (pbk. : alk. paper) | ISBN
    9781421428765 (electronic) | ISBN 142142875X (pbk. : alk. paper) | ISBN
    1421428768 (electronic)
Classification: LCC PS3608.E5855 A6 2019 | DDC 811/.6—dc23
LC record available at https://lccn.loc.gov/2018036807

A catalog record for this book is available from the British Library.

Special discounts are available for bulk purchases of this book. For more information,
please contact Special Sales at 410-516-6936 or specialsales@press.jhu.edu.

Johns Hopkins University Press uses environmentally friendly book materials,
including recycled text paper that is composed of at least 30 percent post-consumer
waste, whenever possible.

For Biddy,
in on the joke

Viola
Thy reason, man?

Clown
Troth, sir, I can yield you none without words; and
words are grown so false, I am loath to prove
reason with them.

Viola
I warrant thou art a merry fellow and carest for nothing.

William Shakespeare, *Twelfth Night*

Contents

BALLYHOO

Spoiler Alert

Stop here if you don't want to know the end

which was, in truth, inevitable: what you thought
was going to happen, happened. If you'd pictured,

in the end, a room, there was a room. If you thought
you'd hear people laughing outside the open window,

there they stood, and in fluttered the beautiful notes.
Whoever you thought would be there, was there.

See? You didn't even have to see it. You could have—
no, you should have—stopped there, in the beginning,

for here it is, the end as you expected, where it always was.

True Story, No Joke

What's so funny? What's so funny?
the man screamed as he slammed

my head again, again, again, again
against the cinderblock wall.

What I was trying to spit out,
blood-choked, I've long since lost.

But all the friends I have left
say it sounded just like *ballyhoo*.

Ballyhoo? The silvery baitfish?
The bombast of the bs'er?

Well, hell. I guess I'll take it.
For in those early speeches

I'm sure I *moo-moo*ed and *choo-
choo*ed and *yaba-daba-doo*ed

to the utter laughing delight
of mother that—small wonder—

I'd return to anything ending
in the oo-oo's of pure pleasure.

What's so funny? What's so funny?
the man kept screaming while I

could not stop laughing, saying
something not (but kin to) *hallelujah!*

> The disaster inherent in being torn away from
> our chosen image of what and who we are in this
> world.
>
> Arthur Miller, "Tragedy and the Common Man"

Comedy and the Uncommon Woman

Chain-smoking, my mother, one-handed, swung
the swing with me in it. It's where I must have learned
her humor, pushed away each time I came back to her.

At last we both laughed, so I jumped, thudded
in sand, then sprung up to see a man—a stranger
not my father—who'd emerged from the park's thicket

and stunk muskily of what even then, unmistakably,
was whiskey. "Your boy," he muttered, "seems so familiar.
Isn't he the missing one I've seen on all the posters?"

The time of the Lord had come, he said, to take me away,
to claim his just reward. He touched me on the shoulder.
How unfunny, I learned, the world can suddenly become.

And there in the high sun of summer, yes, how much colder.
My mother ground her butt down by heel. Lit one.
"Oh," she joked, "that's him all right. And the kidnapper?

She's me." Then my mother laughed her high hard laugh.
I didn't know it then, but then must have been when
I discovered we could have been another—any other,

4

not son and mother, but two strangers gathered together
for no better reason than a joke. And it must have been
when I learned how laughter can disarm, like smoke.

For his part, I saw that man, years later, hawking watches
near a public fountain. But as for my mother? I caught her
just once, I thought—as though off-stage, from inside

a bar I passed. Not her face, which is hard to remember,
and no light shone through the glass. But inside, twice,
like the strikes of a hammer, those—hers—high hard laughs.

That Laugh You Have, or, A Study in the Via Negativa

That laugh you have—although it's close to this—
is not a rustle in the high grass over which

the wind has passed, nor glassy breaker-sets,
shore-crashed, nor glass itself, softly broken

between sheets of felt, nor gull-flocks lifting,
nor any river running over river stones

that bends, brushing willow limbs, and though
I'm getting closer, that laugh you have

is not the green world's mumble, swishes in
the thicket where clumps of trumpet vine,

smilax, and sumac swell, contract perennially,
and which has beckoned me. I was tasked, once,

with searching for the faithful metaphor.
No more. That laugh you have? Nothing's like it.

Playing Cards with Mark Strand

Of this I'm sure:
I wasn't sure.

Perhaps he had
what he hadn't—

two of a kind,
a kind of rhyme,

something that might
suggest the world

less random than
the world of which

he'd written thus
suggests: something,

yes, metrical—
a straight or flush,

but I'd guessed
to call his bluff

because? Because
I too can doubt?

Nothing? No thing?
Or nothingness?

I have nothing,
he said, then laid

his cards face up
so that we saw

he told the truth.
So funny, yes,

how he said it,
so Mark Strand-esque.

I have nothing.
And now we laugh

because? Because
that was something?

Some thing? At least:
somethingness?

Plot Summary

Back then it could have been
what it isn't,

and now the years are less
than sentences,

and now how funny it all seems,
the little street

on which the house once stood.
So easy to read

not too deeply into things.
To say the streets

are empty as pages, the children
have all gone inside.

One might as well speak of storm
clouds gathering.

To make a long story shorter,
I'll start over.

From my window it's very plain:
No children. Clouds.

Reality as Prank

The trees, they told us, were trees.
And we believed. We, pointing, said,
Tree, and they agreed. Then, in turn,
we learned how tree is word, how word
is only air we breathe. Or: dark marks
on a blank page. Tree is no more tree
than you are you. And I am not me.
In time, we grew inclined to disbelieve.
For love is a joke we tell ourselves,
a mere cloak for the libido? And truth?
Beauty? God? Words, words, words.
Absurd. Our best guess? Just simulation.

Even this story of Dostoyevsky—how,
blindly led, he met the firing squad—
smacks of fiction. How he kissed the cross,
took a piss—all this for the last time—
then stood in line until a messenger
arrived to say, well, something along
the lines of a punchline: *Stop this execution.*
Remove the blindfolds. Long live the tsar.

So that was that? A simple waking?
And then there was light, the world

returned, more than word, the trees
defined, and swaying in the distance,
in a kind of slow, underwater silence?
If so: Wake me again, then, in the room
where I no longer lie alone. Speak to me.
Tell me you were kidding. That cruelty
is a joke. That the fragrance of jasmine
drifts in again through the open window.
That the trees are trees. That I am pardoned.

"Forgive Us Our Happiness"

Forgive us this leisure,
this pleasure, this privilege

of vistas we witness
this lavender evening

while sipping our bourbon
as all of the cloudbank

erases the mountains.
Forgive us this wonder:

that whatever we're missing
returns in dissolving—

the ridgelines, a father,
or just all the fall days

we walked by the river
among rhododendron,

believing, in sunlight,
that joy is a blessing.

Is this simply the thinking
such privilege affords us?

Yes, misery always
is happening elsewhere.

Let's hope that what leaves us
is gone then forever.

Return to the present.
The moment's a sentence,

the future no question.
I ask for repentance.

And also: another
two fingers of bourbon.

Recovering the Sunk

The black river's still surface,
like old glass, or, perhaps, a page
of revised fiction, was giving back
the world above us—
> the mossy cypress,
> the sky-set wisps
> of clouds adrift.

But what we wanted was way past that.
We'd snaked through the winter river
not yet full of snakes, and come at last
to what the map didn't show
> was our secret place,
> a dark cove
> in whose bitter cold

we dove, scooting around
and grazing the bottom
until one of us, having found
the mud-sunk log, cried for the winch,
> which, attached,
> made the pontoon
> angle down

and the bubbles rise, and we called that
"the log about to show its face."
For obvious reasons, I thought of how,
when they built Shaw Air Force base,
      they had to move
      a cemetery full
      of glass caskets,

and why would I not picture men
toting shovels in moonlight,
the dirt flung up, the icy sound
of a shovel blade nicking glass,
      or see the hand
      of the bravest man
      reaching down,

smearing away dirt? Or hear the scream
leap from his throat? And then a laugh
of recognition welling up like water?
And when the last laugh dies down,
      that is the sound
      a mud-sunk log
      makes coming up,

its face almost petrified—dense
and ax-hewn, like a pencil
on the river's page. We hollered.
We converted each inch
      into board feet,
      the lumber into
      thousands of dollars—

as good a day as any for men
who hadn't chopped it down,
nor known last century's heat,
its snakes as thick as its lumberjacks' arms.
             Now was the time
             to go upriver
             to the old sawyer's,

to wait six months before it dried.
A hundred years ago, we said, one
of us would have died, then been buried
in a crude box made from yellow pine,
             an unmarked grave
             no hand would touch,
             not ever, in no plot

beside this river whose darkness
contains, always, the unrecovered,
whose surface is like a finish,
the glossy sheen we'd feather on
             for men not us
             to see themselves in,
             and feast upon.

Docent

Our docent jokes: The way ahead
is hellish. Call me ... Virgil.

Of our group, our docent notes:
Has death undone so many?

Really, our docent doesn't,
judging from his past,

expect to get a laugh.
Really, he's a sad man. And ...

nothing in the literature
suggested Literary.

It's History, after all,
we're after—all our, therefore,

skittish laughter, as if
a band of sinners, turning up

at Hell's gates, says: Tell us
you're joking. You're joking, right?

So imagine our surprise when
from the back a woman cries:

Our man's a Dante fan!
Commedia! Canto One!

Our docent jokes: Oh, good God,
now what the hell have I done?

Oh how our docent loves puns.
And oh how we love our docent.

Who asks us: So...you're not dead?
None of us says no. Or yes.

We are silent. Our docent jokes:
Now you're ready to be led!

Freud in 1939

Exiled, he thinks, like storm-mad Lear,
he lies down, watching the rain
fall over London again.

He looks up from *La peau de chagrin*
and calls for his medicine,
wanting little (or nothing) after Balzac

except the slow descent
into a private theater of dreams
a Greek chorus sings.

No more will he revise his theme
than faithfully repent.
His books are burning in Berlin.

He can hear the drumbeats
sounding in the streets
like the onset of a symptom,

and he calls out to Schur for a final smoke.
(How many years past his youth
had the cancer leaked into his mouth?)

His ashtray is empty. Schur arranges
the needles neatly, then says:
But, sir, I thought there are no jokes.

He laughs. The morphine drips.
He thinks that what's ahead
is probably some abyss as deep

as the mind's mysteriousness.
He shuts his eyes and slips
into our memory of last century.

Mr. Hall

In those junior high hallways we always
clung as the late bell long had rung—
like, one later thinks, lovers in Byzantium,
or on a Grecian urn.
                    Here he comes! we murmured,
after we'd unjammed our tongues, unhooked
our thumbs from one another's belt loops . . .
rendered asunder by the thundering voice
booming: *It's Time!*
                    (Now recalling Auden's lines:
*Time watches from the shadows and coughs
when you would kiss.*)
                    Early on in his career
he probably coveted this duty.
                    Truly: Mr. Amorous
Interruptus.
          Monsieur Aubade.
                         Hell, God.
But later, in time, *It's Time!* becomes *There was . . .
a time.*
          I heard he'd slowed, to take his time
and, sometimes, altogether stall.
                    Oh, let love linger

a little longer for the younger...

                                      Was this his thought?

Back then we listened.

                        We knew his gait.

                                That cough.

And so.

        The bell would ring, and on our own then,
before it was time, as though rehearsing for
the losses in our lives to come...

                              we broke it off.

Against Jubilance

When I heard the splash, perhaps,
yes, it was like a laugh,
but nothing else about those deer

crossing the snowy river—
their black noses polished like leather,
their black stony eyes,

the way they leapt up the bank
and grazed lazily in the woods—
was—even remotely—funny.

I've agreed instead with what
my silence said: This was beauty.
And beauty isn't funny.

Funny how funny would be
a more sinister brute—
some drunk, my father, a bear—

I later, elsewhere, could say
had splashed across the river.
But these were only deer,

and they were swimming
together in the snow,
and I witnessed this alone.

This was no laughing matter.
Once, though, I humored myself
and called it jubilance—

that feeling close enough to joy,
to the joy of amusement—
just that—another amusement.

And oh, that was oh-so-close.
But no. If I could take you there,
and show you those deer,

that river as it ran in the snow,
you too would turn and call
the moment beautiful.

And I would ask you,
seriously, exactly what
I thought would be

expected of me: "If one
must speak so plainly,
why say anything at all?"

What We Need Here Is a New Dialect Noun

For the way the strange stain's shape and shade
on carpet changes in late summer light,
that act—*burmba*, maybe?—when morph isn't right,
or metamorphose, or transform, or fade—

and for that moment when the shadow of the gull
and the shadow of the maple tree become,
if noticed, one—maybe *colivirun*—
all collide, the convivial run of a little while . . .

For what we need here, I say, are new sounds
for the things we've missed, as I might say
warnitort, meaning: some sort of way
paper gets crumpled or sheets get wound,

or *harpnim* for that first muted star when
it hangs a fleet half-hour from a hemlock limb.

Reading the Water

Whose livelihood is water, the helmsman
      becomes each day Alexei Karamazov,

poring over, monastically, the facts.
      The tide? Half-slack as Bartleby, the scrivener,

but falling like all things in the Second Coming,
      and only deep as Limbo in the low tide holes.

And the wind? The wind picks up in the morning
      like the poems of Elizabeth Bishop,

and then dies down again, in the late afternoon,
      like the poems of Robert Lowell.

Coaching the Witness

Here's what you've seen, repeat:
shadows
of maple trees mapped
out on the screen,
the steam rising from rain-
drenched cushions,
a skein of milk, a scree of crumb,
and leaf fronds,
though not like open palms
upturned at communion.

You saw (you can call them, yes,
brazen) boulders,
mid-stream, and more
moon-dragged things—
the tidelines, say,
of a paperback bent
back. But

the helmeted planets you didn't see,
nor the preliterate stars,
nor the hangnail moon,

yet you saw the frost,
and it was abrasive,
and you witnessed,
it's true,
an embassy of mountains.

Evade any questions about grief
mushrooming
into laughter, and plead ignorance,
when asked,
about the lily-choked pond.

Stand ground on facts:
you saw how the leaves,
overnight, were gone,
but you can only recall
the clear moon in the cold
as it shone on dark limbs.

All of this you saw,
and so, when
asked, say once more how
you only remember
a dollop,
perhaps, of cloud,
and what you would call
puddle-skin, but,
(remember to say):

It's hard
to say it all exactly,
just how it was.

A Utah man allegedly killed his wife while on a
cruise ship in Alaska, and told a witness he did it
because she wouldn't stop laughing at him, the
FBI said.

CNN

Questions from the Witness

She wouldn't stop laughing? Her laughing went on?
And on? And on? And on? And on? She laughed
ad nauseum? Ad infinitum? No denouement?

He pleaded, Please, stop? What? What have I done?
Her answer like laughter rising in an updraft?
For she wouldn't stop laughing? Her laughing went on?

He went to the railing? He looked to the ocean?
He screamed with the seagulls? He thought of the life raft
ad nauseum? Ad infinitum? No denouement?

Not even a breather? A pause? Not even a yawn?
No word in this world, as though in a photograph?
She can't stop laughing? Or won't? Her laughing goes on?

At him? Or with him? Outside of the joke? Or in on?
Hadn't the joke been that she was his better half . . .
ad nauseum? Ad infinitum? No? Denouement:

Act Five? When the inevitable epiphany comes?
And what then? Call the press? Cue the laugh track?
We can't stop laughing? Our laughing goes on?
Ad nauseum? Ad infinitum? No denouement?

Old Feste, at the Bar, Remembering

"When in all of Illyria I clowned around,
bouncing from alehouse to alehouse,
learning the songs, the ones my father

had not taught me, singing the ones he had,
oh those were the days these days I choose
to refuse to remember, but if asked, perhaps,

when in my cups, by some young comic buck
such as yourself, what it was like, you know,
really like, back then, back when—well,

when what?—and to tell it straight—then I say
you should have been there, young buck,
should have seen then the Illyrian scene,

when the jokes flowed like, well, like wine,
and the wine like jokes, and anything went,
and every punchline had them doubled over

back then, when—as I've said before on stage—
we were witty fools, not these foolish wits,
and humor mended—or patched up—all our bits,

as with the thing I said about Maria being—
recall?—a piece of Eve's flesh—well, it's aged,
not well—quite unfit for this humorless age—

it's like, I've said (you've seen the plays) a glove
turned inside-out, but, hey, I stood there,
at least, center stage, the Great Era of Folly,

back when we weren't always saying sorry
for all the things we said, because words, man,
words were all we had—and me being,

as you know, no routine, juggling, standing-
on-his-head-type jester, no, oh no—
no, man, no, I'm not mad—not, at least,

before my second draft, though funny,
quite funny you should ask, for look—hey—
what say?—I've vented long enough, now,

how about a bit of money—a ten-spot?
a fiver? a twopence? just enough to get
this old fool going? to get him singing again?"

On Taste

Remember the nineties?
Midtown expense accounts,
wide ties, pleats, square-toed shoes,
Twin Towers towering?

Neither do I. I stepped
first foot in The City
too many years later,
at the dizzying height

of the Great Recession,
knowing zilch about,
and having no, money.
My idea of good taste

was still an iceberg wedge—
bleu cheese-drizzled, bacon-
topped, served before a course
of bloody rare prime rib.

Oh, and, of course: Merlot.
Oh, I know that you know.
What we wanted back then
were the familiar forms,

and what's more familiar
than what my mother raved
on and on about, about
all her trips to The City?

Timeless, we said. We said,
classic, first rate, first class.
If you'd have stopped me,
there on Sixth Avenue

and read me my future
like a waiter quoting
the specials, I'd have laughed
you off in a gentle

manly way, with spare change.

Forgetting a Flood

Not even forty days later
and the great event of our time
and place had come and gone.
So began drawdown:

the street-sweeping crews
blew through our heaped keepsakes
neutrally, in the wake
of the news crews tracking

a new storm rolling in
out of the Southwest.
And all the caskets that
(had it really happened?)

once floated like boats down
our streets, were buried again
in rain-freshened griefs.
Now, then, was back to business:

Preachers saw their pews swell up,
then trickle back down again
to the final old believers,
as *Biblical*—the one word

we'd repeated—slipped
from our tongues, not even
falling to the poets,
who for all recent applause

returned to composing
private, secular poems.
And the waterlines faded.
And the dead stayed silent.

To mention, now, The Flood,
meant to laugh, recalling what
to us—alive, unharmed,
unreeling from the footage—

formed another memory
of a time survived—a joke
that burst from the aftermath
into a deeper laughter,

which is like fire, not flood,
which is good, this heat
that helps us (repeat!)
return to forgetting.

Stage Right

Oh those who have
the blessèd right
to be forgotten—
history's means,
the cast aside,
extras, etc., et al.,
all other lords,
messengers, soldiers,
the matronly attendants,
the leather-jacketed
lackeys chewing
on toothpicks,
the company men,
the non-elders
of unstudied tribes;
those not captured
in the delicate light
of any Vermeer
(only in the vague
abstraction here
of my common prayer)
gather and huddle
with my tired father
beyond the pages

of the encyclopedias
he reads at night
and, before sleep,
folds like a bib
on his heaving chest,
snoring away as if
for the crickets outside—
anonymous, too,
like a laugh track.

Thinking I Wanted Country Humor

With cupped hands Jaybo cradled
the owl pellet like a ball of grass

he'd spark for fire, then cracked open
this knickknack of the back woods

where he lived, and said, *Hooters
cough 'em up*, then, *Looks like a turd.*

We always hooted at Jaybo's words—
for what we thought we wouldn't give

to have, like him, grubby fingers
and dirty nails that held the facts

of artifacts: bobtails, arrowheads,
intact antler racks. Inside the owl pellet

he pointed at small skulls and claws,
the bones of rats.
                                        Dawns now,

broken from sleep, I slip out of bed
and hold a cheek to the cold glass

as daylight creeps past the fence
and the piney golf course woods

a hoot owl haunts with his calls:
Who, who are you? Who, who are you?

I am a tired man at a window.
I am no one he wanted to be.

But, oh, for good country humor—
that wit of particulars and new words

I envied, as when Jaybo, years
before he triggered the pistol

held to his head, dug down deeper
in the owl pellet, extracted something

softer—a feather, or maybe a shred
of newspaper—and wriggled it

in our faces, and laughing, told
a joke it took me years and cities

to forget—or, finally, to get. He said,
There's always a worm in the woodshed.

At Slack Tide

Anchored down in a dinghy
at half slack tide,
no clouds, not a stitch of wind,
no verbs, really, of any kind.

And earlier on the incoming
went the joy of the oysters.
And soon on the outgoing
will come the mania of crabs.

But now only noun.
The essence of a thing is this:
sluggishness, mugginess,
a cracking apart, not up.

Until from beyond the fence
of a big blue house on the point
comes a splash, laughter. A pool.
In a pool someone is splashing,

in a big blue house on the point,
in the direction the wind now goes,
the tide turns.
                    If this were a joke,

the punchline might go: Blue is
(wait for it)
the color of the imagination.

After Seeing Four Turtles on a Stump in the Waccamaw River

Just like four old men
I saw once back when
I wasn't happy
and so hightailed it
through small backroad towns
I knew only by signs:
Welcome to Gable,
to Salters, Quinby,
Pamplico, Neeses—
places idleness
fills like half-slack tide
in backwater sloughs
and you say out loud,
Well now, there's a quaint
enough church to fit
smack dab in a film
of slow Southern themes:
some scene with a hot,
windless day in which
the heat's a bad joke
and nothing fidgets
or laughs or cries out
in the anguish of

Achilles after
the death of Patroclus,
which is the sound
of pure poetry.
Not one leaf twitches.
Branches hang heavy.
Maybe a dog barks,
but just once, a half-
bark, on a porch where
a fat man rocks
with his stubbed cigar,
and a box fan whirs.
The kind of town wished
for just in passing,
and I passed through one,
years ago, midweek,
in midafternoon,
in the thick heat of June,
somewhere between where
I was going and
wherever I'd been—
maybe Elloree,
or Pinopolis,
or Plum Branch, or Lane—
and four men sat on
a bench in the shade
and waved and I waved
and I slowed and I thought
to stop, to rest there
for the long dry spell,
not like sloths in hell,
but like turtles on a stump,
that wouldn't budge,

or jump, or splash back
in the black river
whenever I passed.
I thought I'd found
the right town for that,
the right metaphor.
But I kept driving.
I come to the river
years later and see
these turtles on a stump,
just that, and think
back on them, those men
in the shade, and know
nothing but pure
insignificance
in any moment,
or the next—always
a sliding into
wish, forgetfulness,
a trying to get
to someone, somewhere
you don't even know
you won't ever see
again. And the sun
is the same tired sun
lighting the cypress,
that lit the blacktop once.
And that someone for me?
She was, hell, what
I called a dream—
as is how I see
her still, sunbathing
on the green lawn,

idle and dreaming,
as was the way she
waved, so tenderly,
in the light, as was
the way it made me,
I thought then, happy.

Funny Farm

The implements have rusted into curiosities—
clevis, scarifier, scythe.

They hang on the barn walls, or squat up there
on the barn shelves.

We return here to learn and then to forget
the names of things.

Which is to say, we come here merely
to humor ourselves.

And the field of tobacco the one-horse
plough once ploughed

has now literally gone to hay. It's over,
the tour guide jokes,

the heyday. Really (I want to say) it wasn't funny
the first time around.

And out there are some horses whose tails spin
like broken clocks.

And out there we learn that right is Gee, left is Ha,
that Whoa is stop.

Meanwhile, elsewhere, cities go on sprouting
among humorless honks.

Scraping Barnacles from the Hull

Because they had
          attached themselves
to the old hull,

        I laid flat
on my back beneath
        the johnboat

and with a putty
        knife scraped
the barnacles that flaked

        like gray ash
all over my face
        and stuck to

my sweat-damp clothes,
        but on I worked
with the radio blaring

        new songs about
love and work,
        and the day gave

way to now,
        when I'm detached,
still, from a world

        where I will forever
wonder why
        I break myself

breaking into
        song about
work I hated.

The Bait Shop Elegies

1. Captain Squeaky's Bait and Tackle

It was a bait shop town. No one wrote poems.
At dawn, we went, or were drawn to, like fish,
the allure of the live well's thrum, the coffee on.
Then the talk would turn, as it did, to the catch—
the where, the when, the how of it. But what
of the why? Was it the smell—salt-raw fresh—
of the place, the way it'd always been like that,
a musky sea-reek, as if ancient?
Funny you should ask. Yes, dammit, that,
and the tomcat, Mullet, bait-fat, who leapt
up in your lap, and the laminated maps
of the creeks, the sheen of the monofilament,
and the mishmash décor of old crab traps,
cast nets, grubs, jig heads, dangling rigs,
our hook-in-the-bill mesh trucker's caps,
our Little Debbie cakes, our full strength cigs,
our listening to what one captain, Fred, said,
the bottle of Jack, the hacked-up swigs.
When I arrived, Captain Squeaky was dead.
Long dead, they said. *Fifty ticks did him in,*
claimed Fred.
    Ticks? I asked.
         Yep, a hundred,

maybe, itty-bitty fellers bit Squeaky's son
in the deer stand. And that'll make you go,
if you don't know, insane. Fifty ticks and you're done—
something about how no oxygen can flow
to your brain. That boy stabbed his daddy
a dozen times. This little spot on the elbow—
here Fred pinched me—*is what ultimately*
got him.

          No one gasped. We passed
the bottle. We went back to doing what we
always did. Talked of the fishing. Laughed.

2. Big Ed's Tackle Shop

Then Captain Squeaky's brother Ed, Big Ed,
we called him, took over. That was a good run.
Until one morning Big Ed, too, was dead.
Here, basically, is how it all went down:
Big Ed went home to sit, to have a bite
to eat. Old Steve, who'd been around,
said, *And he ain't sat back up. I'm talking White*
Whale, I'm talking Big Tuna, I'm talking . . .
(Old Steve was always talking.) *One night,*
he said, *I had one myself. I was out walking*
and I just fell down. Like this. He gripped
the counter corner. *Look, look. I'm talking*
monster heart attack. Old Steve (all non-descript)
said, *Yep, that's when the doctor stuck*
cow tendon in my heart.

          For that I tipped

the bottle up, said, *Cow tendon? What*
the hell do you mean?

       I mean, don't you scatter
when you hear me moo!

        Well, we erupted
then into what seemed like endless laughter,
until Old Steve said again, *Really, really,*
the last time I went back, I said to that doctor,
"I can't eat steak no more." Doc said, "Too fatty?"
I looked down at my heart. I said, "No, doc!
I don't know if I'm eating mama or daddy!"

And then it was like we would never stop.
And it occurs to me now that our laughter
thrummed like water in that tackle shop.

Pumping the Trout's Stomach

Almost like laughter in a silent film,
that soundless gasping
      prompted when

my father showed me how to pump
the trout's stomach
      so with each laugh

the fish spit out the nymphs and midges,
all the flies we needed for
      imitating

and then presenting—as if no lines
or hooks attached—to the laughing stream
      a parody of

the actual thing, and actually
this time the fish rose, the rod tip
      bent, and father,

let me teach you now what laughter
has meant for me: forgiveness,
      which is release.

Storyboard

In the final episode of our dram-com,
season two, your *Just-shut-the-hell-up*
will shut us up and into unspoken rules
of silence—so that a cough is enough
to set you off, I'll drive off, in the rain,
white-knuckling the steering wheel,
holding an imaginary gun to my brain.
Then I'll pass beneath an overpass and,
for a moment's quiet, the rain will quit.
I'll hover three nights in the blue light
of a cheap motel, listening to a barn owl
you don't believe I've truly seen when
I come home to tell you. But, I'll swear:
This isn't tragic relief. It's true. See how
the camera pans to the face, heart-shaped,
hunkering down on something raw?
Well what (you'll ask) was it like? And
I'll say something stupid like it was like
a flash of light, almost like an insight.
Then we'll figure it out again. We'll cue
the laugh track. Roll the credits. The End.

At the Grave of the Fabulous Moolah

Sick of being called a poet for simply writing poetry
      and wandering in graveyards on sunny Saturdays

like today when a wind blows in as if from the windup
      of your punch, I should like to say today I am retiring

from poetry, effective immediately at the end of this poem,
      but that, going out, I have always wanted to write

a standing-at-the-grave poem because what could possibly
      be more symbolic of retirement than the stillness

of headstones—me out walking and the dead lying down?
      Poetry is a silly thing, so small, and who could imagine

the crowd at a poetry reading yelling, "You ain't shit, Hastings!"
      the way the crowd did in Madison Square Garden, in 1989,

when in black faux-leather boots you stomped Leilani Kai the Hawaiian
      until the announcer, clearly in love with you,

announced, "She gets away with murder!" But how else to heel—
      to be the one everyone loves to hate, risking it all for the sake

of a fake, histrionic art—broken ankle, cracked rib,
   or even, hell, death? Except seeing now how I will never equal that,

I quit. Better to sell insurance, or tend small herbs
   in the garden, or watch children grow old, the reruns on television.

The Comedian Questions Her Timing

At them she throws everything she can,
these humorless men. They never laugh.
Uncanny, really, how unfunny she seems

before them, as though they are a wall
without a flaw or aberration, issuing,
as they do, no guffaw, no cachinnation.

(No, they are not militants. Nor zealots.
Nor, precisely, dead. Dead, yes, serious.
An audience hard, that is, of hearing.)

But isn't all the world the humorous case?
Even now, even here in what she calls, hell,
the darkest and cruelest of recent winters?

Other hilarities: leafless sweet gum trees
laughing like halfwits in benign violations
of half-winds, half-breezes making branches

cackle, the gumballs fall, and almost all
is laughter among applause, it seems,
so why not from them, these humorless men,

why not even the slightest grin you get
sometimes from a corpse, a corpse-grin?
Surely the joke is on her. You got me, she says.

Counterpunch Lines

It is no joke, grief,
so no one says anything,
for there is no punch line
to end this scene and let him
dissolve into laughter after
a man walks into a bar.

It is no joke, loneliness,
the sun rolling up, down,
ad nauseum, Sisyphean,
and the waves forever
repeating themselves to
a man alone on an island.

It is no joke, death,
and the man apologizes
for forgetting, once again,
that it was Halloween
when he answers the door
after no one's knocked.

I felt dizzy and wept, for my eyes had seen that
secret and conjectured object whose name is
common to all men but which no man has looked
upon—the unimaginable universe.

Jorge Luis Borges, "The Aleph"

Sea Pork

No shortage—
here on the shore

of the passing strange—
of the unseen,

though one can't help
but notice *this*—

sea pork—
gelatinous,

lung-colored,
utterly ugly,

so I bend down
and touch it,

as thinking I've
heard laughingly

suggested
by some passerby:

Disgusting!
But I look up

and notice that,
actually,

no one is there,
and I've ceased to exist—

I am just words
and words only—

a character, say,
in a strange book,

who has pocketed
the sea pork

and walked home
from the beach

to peer closely
with a microscope

into the sea pork
and see what? What?

Not his life's aleph—
her freckled hand,

a shark's tooth,
stars in the east,

but nothing—nothing!—
so I try pressing it

like a conch shell
to my ear, to hear

whatever it will give—
the curious laugh

of the porpoise,
Mozart's effusive music,

the erratic crackles
of fire like laughter,

a coffee pot
clearing its throat.

But no. So, I lick it
because it must taste

like something I know
the taste of, though

never have actually
tasted—a Band-Aid,

say, a rubber heart—
but it doesn't taste

like anything,
not even sea pork,

and I remember
I am nothing,

I am only words
in a strange book

you might have read,
once, years ago.

Misfit, Mountain Town

Of him we said he was a character,
our man who lived, as misfits do,
outside of town, in a cabin on a hill,
until, of course, as plotlines go, he then
descended, came around, and we beheld,
as readers do, the realness of our fictions.

For here (it's true) our character had taught
a mouse to sit atop a cat (imagine that!),
but the cat, it sat atop a dog's back
so that the whole three-headed creature
(oh, you would have called it that) walked
about with an heiress' haughty air.

To wit: our ragged preacher even shut
his trap, and beheld, in mute amazement,
what we knew we had here: a true-to-God-
as-our-holy-witness object lesson in
stability. Just imagine, we said,
the possibility! Balance! Harmony!

We laughed and laughed until, of course, as jokes
will go, somebody turned, and said, "Yeah, but.

I heard he trains them with shock collars."

Well.

Well, there went that. We left that town, schooled.
And what remains in memory now? A moral
any half-wit these days gets: Order is cruel.

Sad Clown in the Woods, No Hoax

Envision dawn woods. Little light yet.
A pale whitish blue in the sky evokes
stark oak trunks. Birdcall almost shimmers.
A fog like water creeps beneath the cedars.
Why, of course. This is the way ideas work.

And now a clown. At first you think, yes,
he's not a he but (is it?) just another tree.
No. The light has grown bolder; it shows
his white face, his red nose, a mouth full of
(are they?), yes, yellow teeth. And then his crying,

which is as part of the woods as you are,
as footsteps in leaf-litter, bird chatter,
wolf spiders hopping sideways in deadfall.
Call him over. Oh, here he comes. Your clown
you're summoning out of (is it?) nothing.

No. This is someone. This is a real clown.
The closer he gets, the more you must believe
he is no idea, no metaphor. His shirtsleeves
hang loosely at his elbows. His makeup runs,
from real tears, over his bulbous red nose.

Wanted: The Raccoon on the Dock

At dawn
    I see its
        muddy prints,
the size
    of little-
        neck clams
spackling
    the white boat,
        and know
the raccoon
    is back
        and that while
I slept
    it stuck
        its human-
like hands
    down in
        my minnow traps,
swatting at,
    and eating,
        what I caught
all day
    inside
        the cast net,

drawing
        the net tight
                like a mouth,
    as though
        the net itself
                had an appetite,
    and though
        it's true
                we all have
    appetites,
        to hell
                if that means
    we all deserve
        to go on
                living, so
    I sit as
        still as
                a blue heron
    the next night
        with a .22,
                thinking:
    Let me
        shove
                the carcass
    back in
        my crab trap,
                then toss it
    overboard
        and haul back
                in a dozen
    blue crabs
        I'll crack
                open with

coon-like
      fingers
           to taste
justice,
      its delicate
           meat.

for A. V.

Knuckleheads

More than once
I've fished like slapstick,
a comedy of snags—
hung in the limbs,
dogged the drag,
had the bite turn off
like a joke fallen flat.
Shellcracker,
goggle-eye, warmouth,
stumpknocker, morgan, bream—
easy fishing,
and God knows
that half of the fun
was in the naming, so
I laughed out loud
when you said
you called the fat ones
knuckleheads,
for with what ease
a knucklehead—
whether prompted by
the laughs, or not hearing
them at all—gets
forgiven,

as if born plain dumb,
as if determined from
the get-go
to be gung-ho
for the hook, the joke,
and who else were we too
but two stooges—
buffoonish, cartoonish,
mere caricature
trying to capture
the nostalgic,
picturesque
Norman Rockwell scene
at Cedar Hollow Pond,
where we figured
knuckleheads
surely swam around
just dreaming of our worms
in a world
that, it seemed,
had lightened up enough
to laugh with us: fat flies
all aflutter,
frogs leaping
from the soft mud banks,
and knuckleheads who kept
interrupting
our jokes when
they bit, bent the rod
tips, but who on stringers
in the shallows
had bodies,
sunlit, like oil slicks,

or better yet, like old fools
in particolored
outfits,
flopping and gasping
as if laughing along
at the joke on them.

Ode to a Boat Mechanic

You who no time soon will be bringing me
any sonnets for explication,
dude, I'm telling you, you undeniably
are unimaginably Shakespearean.

I listen. But it's beyond me to get
beyond the words—gearcase, midsection,
impeller, skeg, flywheel, lower unit—
and, like you, into their function.

Brother, you are both word and action,
and I envy, to no end, you for whom a tool
is a tool, is a thing to set things in motion,
as though you played the villain or the fool.

Listen. I'm not calling you evil or dumb.
I'm saying: *You* are the supreme wisdom.

Laughing Gull

How predictably
    the thing observed
        (is a bird)
    then turns to elegy,

for one half expects
    this bird to snap
        the straps
    of its suspenders

the way it dodders
    all befuddled
        like a fat comedian
    before it squawks

and skitters back
    from the waterline
        as if the ocean too
    delivered awkward

silences, as if
    to reconsider—
        for now I'm thinking
    it reminds me

of my funny mother,
>whose wave-like
>>phrases always keep
>rolling back to me:

write something thrilling,
>*something funny,*
>>*write anything*
>*that makes us money.*

I might have
>answered once
>>that birds
>were flight, or song.

I'd be wrong.
>Poetry is about
>>how when you
>look at something

long enough it turns
>to something else,
>>which means
>the thing it once was

is always gone.

Wherever

Rough chop swells from flat calm,
      so the undertow, strong, bobs
            the weak-willed children along,
                  and from the water spits them

staggering into an unfamiliar
      stretch of beach, where, stretched out,
            you see this one wild-eyed child
                  come to you, as though you are her father,

as though—could it be so?—you are a man
      of nurture, and not a drunk who once
            burst like a rat through the door
                  of the wrong home, hunting a party

where you had to go, and how the scene,
      like overwhelming laughter, froze
            and in the television's soft blue light
                  a couple, stretched out on a couch,

jumped up, as though—and could it be so?—
      you were a murderer, but then saw you
            for who you are—no one—and recovered,
                  and fell over into such deep laughter,

welcoming you as though—it could not be so—
      you were the daughter they'd long been
           grieving over, and then how deep you drank,
                for nearly an hour, you remember, now,

leading the child back to where she must go,
      and how they told you as you left them, *Stay*—
           as though—it could not be so—you—
                whoever—could stay wherever, forever.

Hoke

As if his fur had caught on fire,
or the mariachi band had struck up "La Cucaracha,"

or he'd become as death-obsessed
as any dilettantish disciple of Edgar Allan Poe,

the damn dog is on his back again,
rolling around, all up in—what is that?

a duffel bag? a severed head?—so I go over—
no, it's a pelican—and I note what I note—

the (dead) bird's splayed feathers and bones,
its eyes as blank and black as shut-down screens.

No, I cry. *No, no, no, no, no, no, no!*
But the dog knows how hokey I've become.

Nothing I could say would matter now
except as self-instruction, or secret.

Old Billy Yeats was wrong. Song's too easy.
Better to be an animal knowing no pity.

Better to be a ditch-digger, a stone-scrubber,
the garbage man who said to me:

One time, when I took off this lid, I found
a decapitated cat, and, man, I saw its head

wiggling where the maggots had got it.
It was like something independent of itself.

God, that makes me sick it's so appropriate.
I'm all pity. I'm all words. To make my point

I lie down. I wiggle around. I make no sense.
Except: the dog—now curious—gets up,

gets close, and nudges me as if to suggest,
with his dead bird breath, that the fire is out,

or the song is over, or that playtime is up
for men, like me, their death-obsessed poetry.

The Funny Pages

Before the day would break them for work,
or school, and the years break them for good
(so that, looking back, they'd refer to themselves
always in the third person)—there they are,
the family huddled at the breakfast table,
each to one newspaper section as if tasked.
Of course, the father reads the sports.
And the cereal-slurping son is all laughs
at something in the funnies. The mother smokes.
She turns, as always, to the obituaries
like a game. Each day, it seems, she recognizes
another name, and she jokes it won't be long
before hers appears—she rankles the page—
here. The father pleads, *Please. Not again.*
Then—at some dumb thing done by dumb men
like Hagar or Dagwood, perhaps; or, simply,
because his mother's funny—the son laughs.

Throwbacks

Nothing delicious
    this lizardfish
with its thinned
    scale-less skin
or the silver flash
    of the ribbonfish
dangled in the sun
    over the pier.
Nothing here more
    salt could cure:
hardheads, piggy
    perch, grunts,
all of it too gross
    for our tongues.
Nothing so jazzy
    as the clownfish,
the harlequin bass.
    Plainly: trash
to throw back,
    a valid act,
all spasm and thrash,
    as with the past,
to practice, thus,
    the art of release,
to let shit go.

> Lucky the breeze was setting away from the house,
> so it wasn't until well into the morning. But soon
> as I see them it was like I could smell it in the field
> a mile away from just watching them, and them
> circling and circling for everybody in the county to
> see what was in my barn.

William Faulkner, *As I Lay Dying*

As I Lay Dying Laughing

The buzzards were circling
to peck at the mother's flesh—
I read—and my professor said,

That's a lightening effect,
and I heard (how absurd)
That's a lightning effect,

and thus the words fused:
the black flash of bird-bolt—
a symbol of sudden arrival.

I thought I'd learned enough
of literary stuff to know:
sudden arrivals mean Death,

yes, with a capital D—my own,
my mother's and my father's—
and, later, I laughed because

I got the joke: the mother was dead,
and one letter is the difference
between laughter and slaughter,

and one moment it's one summer
at the lake with my mother
watching lightning over the cove,

and the next moment I'm alone,
by a window, recalling
as a flock of blackbirds cry out

in a cloudless sky above me,
how none of this is funny.
No, none of this is funny at all.

Any Which Way You Cut It

Whatever the Dole® watermelon meant—
when I split and bit into it—if I'd bought into
The Myth, as if by The Myth we meant
the corporate clickbait ideal of Americana
continually fattening the factory farm, well,
true that.

And even if the summer day was, I said,
a bluebird day, and what I said was cliché,
for language is mostly fossil anyway, well,
true that, too.

And in spite of the probability that everything
about that summer—fruit, table, sky, view,
me, you, us—was simply simulation,
all a game, a matrix of information, well,
true, true, true.

But can I tell you something? It's not even
a secret. It was damn sweet to have the juice
run down our fingers, to say I love you,
to lean back and look into a sky we agreed,
truly, was blue.

Nothing Liquid, Fragile, Hazardous, Perishable

Far from the creek running
crookedly with
boulders sunlight emblazons.

Yet something hard to grasp,
like my name on the tongues
of those who've forgotten me.

Perhaps like the upturned stern
of a beached skiff
the wind scourges, waves punch.

Still, nothing as haunting
as the stiff body
of an indigo bunting, if

close enough, though not,
the moth wing
I picked up in leaf-rot,

the husk of the cicada I found,
as a child, once,
still clinging to a poplar.

No, just this letter made
of letters, trying
to capture in some material

thing the moment after
laughter, or rapture,
after body or song—

the thing not fully gone.
But isn't it
just a thrum, or a stupor?

And, besides, the cicada husk
was brittle and perfectly
crisp to the point I could not

not bite into
it, and so,
I bit. I swallowed.

I cracked myself up.
I knew, right then,
I was onto something.

Picasso, *Seated Harlequin,*
The Metropolitan Museum of Art

To a Seated Harlequin

Not if when
        but now that
we've grown so fat
        with our bellies full
of barrel laughs
        and cloaked ourselves
in sugarcoats,
        donned the madcaps,
when the punchlines
        are pre-facts,
for to say a thing
        is to make it so,
by way of joke,
        now is the time,
O my ponderous,
        dolorous clown
of Pablo Picasso,
        simply to exist.
The possibilities
        are probabilities.
They're limitless.
        Why bother with
being a thing
        just line and color?

If all of us
        are clowns—then what?—
no one's a clown?
        I say: Stand up.
Step beyond
        the borders where
the present is.
        Revel with me
in the curiously epic
        bliss of becoming
made for this.

Acknowledgments

Grateful acknowledgement is made to the editors of these journals, wherein some of these poems first appeared: *Birmingham Poetry Review*, *Connotation Press*, *SC Voices: Poetry and Prose*, *storySouth*.

I would also like to thank the following people: Lee and Huck, always and foremost; my family; my Sewanee family; the good folks at Coastal Carolina University; everyone at Johns Hopkins University Press; Sidney Wade, A. E. Stallings, and Mark Jarman for close reads; my friends Will Griffin, Jolly Roger, and Adam Vines, for the continued inspiration and the many laughs.

Once again, especially, with eternal gratitude: Wyatt Prunty and Paul Ragan.

Poetry Titles in the Series

John Hollander, *Blue Wine and Other Poems*

Robert Pack, *Waking to My Name: New and Selected Poems*

Philip Dacey, *The Boy under the Bed*

Wyatt Prunty, *The Times Between*

Barry Spacks, *Spacks Street, New and Selected Poems*

Gibbons Ruark, *Keeping Company*

David St. John, *Hush*

Wyatt Prunty, *What Women Know, What Men Believe*

Adrien Stoutenberg, *Land of Superior Mirages: New and Selected Poems*

John Hollander, *In Time and Place*

Charles Martin, *Steal the Bacon*

John Bricuth, *The Heisenberg Variations*

Tom Disch, *Yes, Let's: New and Selected Poems*

Wyatt Prunty, *Balance as Belief*

Tom Disch, *Dark Verses and Light*

Thomas Carper, *Fiddle Lane*

Emily Grosholz, *Eden*

X. J. Kennedy, *Dark Horses: New Poems*

Wyatt Prunty, *The Run of the House*

Robert Phillips, *Breakdown Lane*

Vicki Hearne, *The Parts of Light*

Timothy Steele, *The Color Wheel*

Josephine Jacobsen, *In the Crevice of Time: New and Collected Poems*

Thomas Carper, *From Nature*

John Burt, *Work without Hope: Poetry by John Burt*

Charles Martin, *What the Darkness Proposes: Poems*

Wyatt Prunty, *Since the Noon Mail Stopped*

William Jay Smith, *The World below the Window: Poems 1937–1997*

Wyatt Prunty, *Unarmed and Dangerous: New and Selected Poems*

Robert Phillips, *Spinach Days*

X. J. Kennedy, *The Lords of Misrule: Poems 1992–2001*

John T. Irwin, ed., *Words Brushed by Music: Twenty-Five Years of the Johns Hopkins Poetry Series*

John Bricuth, *As Long As It's Big: A Narrative Poem*

Robert Phillips, *Circumstances Beyond Our Control: Poems*

Daniel Anderson, *Drunk in Sunlight*

X. J. Kennedy, *In a Prominent Bar in Secaucus: New and Selected Poems, 1955–2007*

William Jay Smith, *Words by the Water*

Wyatt Prunty, *The Lover's Guide to Trapping*

Charles Martin, *Signs & Wonders*

Peter Filkins, *The View We're Granted*

Brian Swann, *In Late Light*

Daniel Anderson, *The Night Guard at the Wilberforce Hotel*

Wyatt Prunty, *Couldn't Prove, Had to Promise*

John Bricuth, *Pure Products of America, Inc.*

X. J. Kennedy, *That Swing: Poems 2008–2016*

Charles Martin, *Future Perfect*

Hastings Hensel, *Ballyhoo*